For my parents, Rik and Brigitta, with lots of love
MS

For Anna, Auke, and Koen
MvH

Copyright © 2005 by Lemniscaat b.v. Rotterdam

Originally published in the Netherlands under the title *Bang Mannetje* by Lemniscaat b.v. Rotterdam
All rights reserved—CIP data available

Printed and bound in Belgium

First U.S. edition

Mathilde **Stein** • Mies **van Hout**

Brave Ben

Front Street 8 Lemniscaat

"I am such a coward," Ben said to himself. "When someone pushes ahead of me in line at the bakery, I don't say anything. When I wear my favorite pair of flowered overalls, I'm scared of being laughed at. And when I hear strange noises at night, I think it's a spook under my bed. I need help."

Ben looked in the Yellow Pages under
"Help for Cowards." He found the
listing "Magic Tree." The ad said,
"By appointment only. Success
guaranteed."

Magic! That's just what I
need, thought Ben. He
called to make an
appointment.

The next morning Ben walked to the wild, dark forest where the magic tree lived. "I am in the wild woods with all of the wild, weird creatures," the tree had said on the phone. "But they are harmless, so don't be afraid."

It was a good thing the magic tree had warned Ben. On the way into the forest, a dreadful dragon suddenly appeared. He fumed big clouds of smoke through his nose. Every now and then he spit fire.

"Where do you think you are going?" the dragon roared. Ben could only gulp. Then he remembered that the magic tree had told him not to be afraid. So he looked right into those yellow dragon eyes and said, "Hello, Dragon. I am going to see the magic tree. I have an appointment."

To Ben's surprise the dragon answered very politely, "Walk right through. Take a left at the third swinging skeleton. Please give my regards to the magic tree."

As soon as Ben entered the forest, he heard a loud hissing noise…

...and before he realized what was happening, he found
himself hanging upside down from a spider's web.

An enormous hairy spider crawled toward him. "Mmm," she hissed, "my favorite food!"

It was a good thing Ben knew the spider was harmless. Otherwise he would have been scared to death. "Hello, Spider. Would you untie me, please? I have to meet the magic tree."

"Oh," said the spider, sighing. "That's a pity." But she untied all the knots. "Tell the magic tree that his scarf is almost finished," she said. "And have a good trip."

Ben walked on through the forest.
It was so dark that he could not
see the path. Finally he saw an
arrow with the words "Magic
Tree" on it, but at that very
moment an ice-cold
hand gripped his
neck.

Shocked, Ben turned around. An ugly witch stood behind him. Spiders and cockroaches hung in her hair. She smelled bad and her eyes sparkled spitefully. "What are you doing in my garden?" she cackled.

Yikes! Ben thought. It's a good thing I know she won't do anything horrible. "Good day, madam," he said politely. "I didn't know I was walking in your garden. I am on my way to the magic tree."

"Oh," said the witch. "No damage done. Here's a pumpkin for the magic tree. It will make a lovely pie."

Ben walked on, further into the forest. Bats flitted around his head and he heard wolves howling and other terrible screams, but he did not pay attention to any of that. He took a left at the third swinging skeleton.

There was the magic tree—large and important-looking.

"Hello, Magic Tree," Ben said. "I am Ben. I have an appointment ..."

"Well," said the magic tree. "Did you not see the dragon?"

"Oh yes," Ben said. "He asked me to give you his warmest regards."

"No trouble with the spider?"

"Not at all. She has almost finished knitting your scarf."

"And the witch?"

"She gave me this pumpkin to bring to you," Ben replied.

"Ah," said the magic tree. "Well, well. Hm. Uh. Er. Wellllll ..."
And then he didn't say anything for a long time.

Finally he asked, "How can I help you?"

"I want to be less afraid," Ben said softly.

The tree nodded. Then he said solemnly, "That has already
been taken care of by all that has happened today. You are
now truly brave."

Ben was happy on his way home. He was thinking, What a wonderful tree that is. It has changed me as if by magic into Brave Ben. Now I will never be a scaredy-cat again.

At home Ben changed into his favorite pair of flowered overalls and went to the bakery.

"I am sorry, but I was first," he told a girl who tried to cut in front of him.

He bought two cakes. One for himself, and one for the spook under his bed.